George Wither

Extracts from Juvenilia

George Wither

Extracts from Juvenilia

ISBN/EAN: 9783744716277

Printed in Europe, USA, Canada, Australia, Japan

Cover: Foto ©Andreas Hilbeck / pixelio.de

More available books at **www.hansebooks.com**

EXTRACTS

from

JUVENILIA *or* POEMS
by
GEORGE WITHER

You enchanting Spells that lye
Lurking in sweet Poesy.

Wither.

LONDON:

Printed by GEORGE BIGG, 1785.

Sold by J. SEWELL, *Cornhill*; and J. DEBRETT,
opposite *Burlington House, Piccadilly.*

DEDICATION.

To ————

There is naturally in the human mind a ſtrong diſpoſition to admire TRUTH ; an *exact* repreſentation pleaſes in a picture, even when the things repreſented are, in themſelves, unintereſting : But, whatever brings to remembrance the Objects that are dear, in our affections or reſpect, is a perpetual ſource of exalted pleaſure on Earth.

If *You* had been unknown to me, *Wither's* Poem of " FAIR VIRTUE" would have given me much

leſs

lefs pleafure than it has; I fhould then have read
it only as an elegant defcription of an *ideal Being*:
but the many traits in your character, which bear
a ftriking refemblance to the fineft parts of his defcription, bring that defcription home to the Heart,
as the Picture of *Truth*, and not of *Fancy*.

Every one who knows *You*, will join in the *Poet's*
exclamation

    " Can I think, the *Guide* of *Heaven*,

    " Hath fo bountifully given,

    " Outward features, 'caufe He meant,

    " To have made lefs excellent,

    " Your divine part? or fuppofe

    " *Beauty, Goodnefs* doth oppofe;

                         " Like

" Like thofe Fools, who do defpair,

" To find Any, *Good*, and *Fair ?*

" Rather, there I feek a mind

" Moft excelling, where I find

" God hath, to the body, lent

" Moft-befeeming Ornament.

——— ———

" And I do believe it true,

" That, as we the *Body* view

" Nearer to Perfection grow :

" So, the *Soul* herfelf doth fhow :

" Others more and more excelling,

" In her powers ; as in her dwelling."

Altho' fit fubject for comparifon may be found
in *Your Perfon* ; it is from the *Poet's* defcription of

the

the *Mind* and *Behaviour*, whence an idea, of perfect similitude, arises in the imagination of

Your most devoted

30th *May*, 1785.   *Aretephil.*

INTRO-

INTRODUCTION.

THE intention of this *Publication* is, to diffuſe that pleaſure, which the Editor has enjoyed from the peruſal of *Wither's* POEMS, by promoting a *Republication* of the JUVENILIA, in caſe the Publick Curioſity ſhould be incited, to recover from obſcurity theſe, almoſt forgotten, POEMS.

The Editor will venture to ſay that The *Poem* "FAIR VIRTUE, The Miſtreſs of Philarete." contains a more perfect Syſtem of Female Tuition than is any where elſe to be found. *Wither's* Pen flows as freely with becoming praiſe, as biting Satyre; and was always employed in the cauſe of Virtue: There is, in his Works, uⁱcommon ſtrength of mind, and peculiarity of thought, often moſt happily expreſt.

The

The Editor having mentioned, in the courfe of this Publication, *Wither's* HALELUIAH, he cannot refift tranfcribing two pieces from it; The one an anniverfary ejaculation of a happy Couple: The other an annual Tribute to the Memory of a departed Friend.

" For anniverfary Marriage-days.

LORD, living, here are we
As faft united, yet,
As when our Hands, and Hearts by Thee,
Together, firft were knit,
And, in a thankful *Song*,
Now, fing we will Thy Praife,
For, that Thou doft as well prolong
Our *loving*, as our *Days*.

Together we have now,
Begun another year;
But, how much time Thou wilt allow,
Thou maks't it not appear.

We,

We, therefore, do implore,
That *live*, and *love*, we may,
Still fo, as if but one day more,
Together we fhould ftay.

Let each of others *wealth*,
Preferve a faithful care,
And of each other's *Joy* and *Health*;
As if one Soul we were.
Such confcience let us make,
Each other not to grieve,
As if we, daily, were to take
Our *Everlafting-Leave.*

The *frowardnefs*, that fprings
From our *corrupted-kind*,
Or from thofe troublous *outward-things*,
Which may diftract the mind ;
Permit Thou not, oh LORD,
Our conftant Love to fhake ;
Or, to difturb our true accord ;
Or, make our hearts to ake.

But

But let thefe *Frailties* prove
Affection's Exercife:
And, that Difcretion, teach our Love.
Which wins the nobleft prize.
So, *Time,* which wears away
And ruins all things elfe,
Shall fix our Love on Thee for aye,
In whom, *Perfection*, dwells."

" For an anniverfary Funeral-day.

The Day is now return'd
Which in memorial of my *Friend*
(When firft for her I mourn'd)
To fet apart I did intend.
'Tis now a year,
Since for my *Dear*,
This yearly *Rite* was done;
And, I as yet,
Do not forget
My loffes to bemoan.

I muft

I muſt indeed confeſs
That (tho' to LOVE, ſtill, true I am)
My *Paſſions* now are leſs:
And, that my Grief is not the ſame;
For, *Time* aſſures
More perfect cures,
When *Sorrow* woundeth man,
Than all the pow'rs
Of Herbs and Flow'rs,
Or *Human-Reaſon* can.

Thy *Name*, oh GOD, I praiſe
That, Thou, by *Time*, haſt eas'd me ſo:
For, doubtleſs, length of days,
Without Thy *Mercy*, lengthens *Woe*.
When Thou doſt pleaſe,
From *Pain*, to *Eaſe*,
We in a night return.
And when we grieve,
Thou muſt relieve,
Or, we ſhall ever mourn.

That yearly *Rite*, therefore,
Which to my *Friend*, my paſſion vow'd;
Shall honour her the more,
If, on Thy praiſe, it be beſtow'd,
And, if this Day
Will paſs away
In thankful thoughts of Thee;
Which once I meant
To have miſpent,
In Griefs that fruitleſs be.

Nor is my *Friend* forgot
Tho' thus I turn from her to Thee:
The leſs I love her not,
Tho' now I ſing Thy love to me.
Whilſt Thee I mind,
In Thee I find
My *Friend* again reviv'd:
When *her* alone,
I think upon,
I, for one *dead*, am griev'd.

The

The Virtues of this *Friend*,
Within myſelf let me improve;
And to that noble End,
Cauſe her memorial me to move.
For, if we ſtray,
From their Juſt-way,
Whom we in Life approv'd;
Thoſe whom we ſeem'd
To have eſteem'd,
We never truly lov'd

LORD, I am drawing near,
To her Eſtate whom I bemoan;
Yea, nearer by a year,
Than when this duty laſt was done.
And ſtill I come
The farther from
The State I did deplore;
As nearer to
That State, I grow
Which equals *Rich* and *Poor*.

Vouchſafe,

Vouchfafe, oh GOD ! I pray,
That hence remov'd when I fhall be,
In Thee behold I may,
All thofe that were belov'd of me.
Yea, let none here,
To me be dear,
But thofe whom I fhall find,
Enjoy that Love,
In Heaven above,
Which they, on Earth, fhould mind.'"

The Editor's Avocations do not admit him to
undertake the *Republication* of *Wither's* JUVENILIA
but he would not hefitate to communicate his copy
to a proper Perfon for that purpofe.

THIS, almoſt forgotten *Poet*, GEORGE WITHER
or *Wyther*, was born on 11th June 1588 and
died 2d May 1667.

His early Works were much admired, as appears
from the various editions of them : in his *Fragmenta
Prophetica*, it is ſaid, that about *thirty thouſand*
copies of " *His Motto*" printed in 1618, were
ſold in a few months ; altho' this *Poem* is now
ſcarcely to be found : The Editor has *two different
Editions* of it in 8°. printed in 1621 : and another in
the 12°. Edition of the *Juvenilia* 1633.

The JUVENILIA is a *Collection* of *Poems*, before
publiſhed, written by *George Wither* ; the 12°.
Edition is dated 1633 : but this Collection was of
an earlier date viz 1622, in 8°.

The Copy of the 8° Edition, in the Editor's
poſſeſſion, wants the *engraved Frontispiece*, which is

A   the

the *Title-Page*, but the following introductory verses are prefixed to " *Abufes ftript* and *whipt*," both in the 8°. Edition of 1622, and the 12°. Edition of 1633.

To the READER,

Upon thefe Poems

THESE JUVENILIA (or thefe *youth-paftimes*)
Set forth in homely and unpolifht *Rhimes*,
Let none defpife : For, whatfoe'r they feem,
They have their *fate*, their *ufe*, and their *efteem*,
And will be read ; when thofe, more feeming wife,
Have far lefs ufe, and fhorter Deftinies.
Nor, read you them, with that cenforious eye,
As if you look'd for curiou'ft *Pcefy*.
If that be fought for, others can afford
Large *Volumes*, and with *Art*, far better ftor'd.
And, this our *Author* anfwers your defire,
If for his riper labours you enquire.

Here

Here, you fhall fee what *Nature* could impart,
Ere he had Time, or Means, to compafs *Art*:
What *Strains* a native honefty could reach;
What knowledge and what boldnefs it can teach:
And, that in TRUTH, a majefty there is,
Tho' mafked in difpifed *fimplenefs*.

Among the *Learn'd*, this *Author* had no name,
Nor did he this way think to purchafe Fame;
For, when he This compofed, it was more,
Than he had read in twice twelve months before;
And by his latter ftudies, fome difcern,
That, firft he writ, and then began to learn,
Be't what it will: 'tis that, he means fhall pafs,
To fhew how foolifh, and how wife he was.

No *Critick* now, doth in thefe *Poems* fee,
A blemifh, or a fcape, more foon than he:
He knows as well as they, what feems amifs
In thefe *Inventions*; and what childifh is.
He knows how far they differ from thofe *lays*,
By which the learned *Poet* hunts for praife:

And

And wherein thofe abfurdities do lye,
Which (to their thinking) mar his *Poefy*.
And, yet, he will not mend them: For his *name*
Is loved more, and higher flyes his fame,
By thefe defpifed *Numbers*, than their *pride*
Can raife them yet, who did his lines deride.
And, that his *Matter* will be priz'd, he knows ;
When their fil'd language out of fafhion grows.

    Thus therefore, uncorrected and untrim'd,
You have thefe *Poems*, as they firft were limn'd :
Which (tho' fome may diflike) fome will approve,
For, many men will leave a pruned Grove,
And curious Garden-allies, to go fee,
What pleafures in untilled Mountains be :
And much delight in Woods to take the fhade,
Of artlefs Arbours, by rude Nature made.

    Befide; as there be many men, who long
To fee of what complexion being young
Their Bodies were ; and to that purpofe fave,
Unalter'd, thofe their Pictures which they have.

                   So

So, he, thus having drawn (as here you find)
In childiſh years the picture of his *mind*,
Unalter'd, leaves it; that in time to come,
It may appear how much he changeth from
The ſame he was: And, that, befeen it may,
How he *amends, grows worſe*, or *keeps a-ſtay.*
Then, whether he could better this or no,
His purpoſe is, ſome other way to ſhow.

It is not eaſy to determine what the JUVENILIA
properly comprehends; The Editions of 1622 and
1633 agree, in lettering the ſheets fucceſſively from
" *Abuſes ſtript and whipt*" to the *end* of " The
" *Shepherd's Hunting*:" in the Edition of 1633, the
pages are continued to the *end* of " Fidelia;" but
not lettered, and its particular Title-Page is dated
1632: in the Edition of 1622 " Fidelia" is neither lettered nor paged, tho' dated 1622. "*Wither's*
" Motto" is in both volumes; but *not paged* in
either; and lettered by itſelf in both. In the 8°.
Edition, the *former pieces* are printed for *John Eudge*

and

and "*Wither's Motto*" for *John Marriot* : in the 12°.
Edition the *former* for *Robert Allot* and the "*Motto*"
for *John Grifmond* : " The Miftrefs of Philarete" is
not in the 8°. volume ; but whether accidentally
deficient in the copy which the Editor poffeffes, or
omitted in the collection, does not appear, tho'
there is no catch word to indicate its having ever
been in the Volume : in the 12°. Edition it is con-
nected to the " *Motto*" by a catch word, and as it
is preceded by a preface of *John Marriot*, tho'
printed for *John Grifmond*, *it* is moft probably re-
printed by *Grifmond* from a former Edition, by
Marriot, as well as the " Motto."

      Wood (Athen. Oxon) fays that
  " Iter Hibernicum, or Irish Journey
  " Iter Bor: or Northern Journey
  " Patrick's Purgatory   } written in
  " Philarete's Complaint   verfe
 " were called the JUVENILIA"

                                         Wood

Wood is demonstrably wrong, concerning the *Contents* of the JUVENILIA; and therefore a doubt must remain, whether the *Poems*, mentioned by him, are the Works of *Wither*. " Philarete's Complaint" called in the early Editions of " Abuses stript and whipt" *Arctophil's Complaint*, is alluded to by the *Poet* himself, but the *others* do not appear any where to be even hinted at. *Wood* adds that he had never seen " *The Mistress of Philarete*" so that it is incertain whether " *Philarete's Complaint*" and " The " *Mistress of Philarete*" be the same Poem under different names, or different Poems.

In two Copies, which the Editor has seen, of the 12°. volume, the contents are the same, viz.

Abuses

various Editions

" Abuſes ſtript and whipt (1611*)1613, 2 Edit. 12°.
(1614, 8°.)1615, 12°. 1617,
12°. 1622, 8°. 1633†, 12°.

Prince Henry's Obſequies(1612, 4°.)1617, 12°. 1622,
8°. 1633, 12°,

A Satyre to the King   1614, 12°.(1515, 8°)1616,
12°. 1622, 8°. 1633, 12°.

Epithalamia   .   .   1622, 8°. 1633, 12°.

The

---

* Mr. *Herbert* has a copy of " Abuſes ſtript and
whipt," wanting the *Title-Page*, with *Wither's Head*
1611 ætat: ſuæ 21 —÷— 1588 = 1609; ſo that 1611 muſt
relate to the *Publication*, and *not* to *Wither's age*. The
copy at the *Britiſh Muſeum*, of the Edit. 1615, has
Wither's Head, but the Pages are 302, in Mr. *Herbert's*
344; ſo that they cannot be the ſame Edition.

† Book 2d is dated 1633, certainly an error of the
Preſs.

The Shepherds Hunting 1615, 2 Edit. 12°. [1620*,]
1622, 8°. 1633, 12°.

Fidelia

---

* It is fufpected there is a *miftake* here; for fome
Stanzas quoted from this Edition of " The *Shepherd's Hunting*" are not in either of the Editions of
1615, nor in thofe of 1622 and 1633: It is therefore
very unlikely They fhould be found in an intermediate
Edition of 1620, if there was fuch an Edition, which
may be doubted, for The *Stanzas* fo quoted from
" The *Shepherd's Hunting*" are really in " The
" *Miftrefs of Philarete*," The Stationer in a Poftfcript to " The *Miftrefs of Philarete*" mentions that
" fome of the *Sonnets* in *It*, had been before printed
" in the imperfect and erroneous copy foolifhly en-
" titled his Works." Perhaps this imperfect and
erroneous Edition may be what is referred to, as
bearing date 1620. The *Stanzas*, in that quotation,
are *not all*, which " The Miftrefs of Philarete" contains.

Fidelia	(1619, 8°) 1622*, 8° 1632†, 12°
Wither's Motto	(1618), 1621†, 2 Edit. 8° 1633, 12°
Fair Virtue, The Miſtreſs of Philarete }	(1622, 8°) 1633, 12°
Epigrams, Sonrets, Epi- taphs, &c. }	1633, 12°

N. B. Thoſe Editions in Parentheſes The Editor has not ſeen, the others are in his poſſeſſion.

If

---

* To Fidelia" are added " Paraphraſes on the Creed and Lord's Prayer" not paged.

† The date 1632 is probably an error of the Preſs for 1633, as the pages are continued from " The " Shepherds Hunting" thro' " Fidelia."

‡ The Title Page to " *Wither's Motto*" is engraven and bears the date 1621; but the Copy with the Collection of 1622, may have been printed in that year, as the other pieces are, tho' the date was not altered in

the

IF POETRY be the POWER of COMMANDING the IMAGINATION, conveyed in *meafured language* and *expreffive epithets*, WITHER was truly a POET. Perhaps there is no where to be found, a greater variety of *Englifh Meafure* than in His Writings; (Shakefpear excepted) more Energy of Thought, or more frequent developement of the delicate filaments of the Human Heart.

One

---

the Plate. The affertion, therefore, of *two different Editions* 1621, may be doubtful; and all that can be pofitively faid, is, that there are two different Editions S^o. of 1621, or 1621 and the fubfequent year. The other Copy, in poffeffion of the Editor, appears to be antecedent to that bound up with the Collection of 1622, as the *Poftfcript* is *added* to this laft : the former, by the impreffion of the Copper Plate, appears, however, *not* to have been the *Firft Edition*, as the Plate is much worn. They are printed page for page, but with typographical differences.

One modern Verſifier complained that *Wither's* verſe was *rough*; On the other hand, a Lady, who is Miſtreſs of all the modulation of ſweet ſounds, admired how the lines run into each other, with the beauty of blank verſe, without loſing the ſpirit of the lyrick meaſure: Attention to the Old Engliſh Poets will clearly ſhew, that there was a greater variety admitted, in pronunciation and accent, than is allowed in modern verſification: The Ear which cannot conform itſelf to the antient practice, but is bound in the Silken Traces of modern verſe, may be offended, ſometimes, with the early Poets; and, in every reader it will require a habit and uſe before the Ear attains the compleat practice, without which many lines will appear *proſaic*. Words alſo become *obſolete*; or what is worſe, appropriated to vulgar Ideas *only*: ſuch will ever be a ſtumbling block to a reader without Genius.

Mere Verſifiers frequently ſtile themſelves *Poets*, but the recital of common ideas, in however flowing language, can never, with propriety, be ſtiled *Poetry*;

Poetry; nor does the moſt exact deſcription of Nature, of Man or Manners deſerve the name, unleſs that deſcription raiſes, in the imagination, ſome idea not expreſſed ; and if it does, nothing can be ſo trivial as not to give pleaſure to a mind of quick conception: An apt example occurs in " *The* " *Shepherd's Hunting*."

" I with wonder heard thee ſing
" At our laſt year's revelling :
" Yea I ſaw the Laſſes cling
" Round about thee in a ring ;
" As, if each one jealous were,
" Any but Herſelf ſhould hear."

The art of aſſigning a fanciful reaſon for an ordinary action is the Soul of Poetry: we can here imagine the *countenances* of the *encircling auditory :* The Imagination muſt ever be the Poet's Commentator: and Its ſcope is univerſal, embracing the World of Ideas as well as Forms: It may happen hat a man ſhall be ſo deſtitute of Imagina.

B   tion

tion, as to have no relish for *true Poetry*, and prefer mellifluous verses; but the want of sight does not prove that there are no Colours in the Rainbow. They who are *satisfied*, for *pleased* none can be, with the flowing lines of those modern versifiers, who have fewer ideas, of their own, than the *learned Pig*, are not the People for whom the *repast* of *Wither's Poems* is adapted: Lovers of natural thought and sentiment will be pleased at being brought to acquaintance with *Wither*: but to enable them to judge for themselves was the intention of the Specimens which follow: they are taken from *different Poems*, to convey, to those who are ignorant of the *Poet*, an idea of what they may expect: but scarce any of these quotations are compleat; the intention of them being to *raise*, and *not* to *satisfy*, Curiosity.

In some of his latter pieces, *Wither* has given up the reins to Enthusiasm, and is rather to be considered as displaying himself in the character of a *Prophet*, than a *Poet*: neither these, nor his *Political Poems*, come within the intention of this publication;

tion; altho' many fine things are interfperfed in his *Haleluiah, Campo-Mufæ*, and in his other pieces not here recited: in the *Haleluiah* there are fome things, perhaps, no where to be furpaffed.

Wither's Prophetical and Political Poems feem to have been the true caufe of that depreciation of his merit, which we find broached by his Cotemporaries, and retailed in fubfequent writers.

· *Swift* has ftigmatized *Wither* in his Battle of the Books; but as *Dryden* is joined with him, the opprobium falls on the *Critick* and not on the *Poets*: for it is too abfurd to be allowed in the candour of criticifm, that condemnation fhould be paft on *Alexander's Feaft*, The *Origin* of *Harmony*, or *Abfalom* and *Achitophel*, becaufe their Author, in his Plays, publifhed much trafh, that has been fo juftly ridiculed by the *Rehearfal:* The value of Poets muft be tried by the fame ftandard as the Metallick Ores; by the proportion of the finer metal to the drofs: and, in the aggregate Mafs, a *Grain* of *pure Gold* is of more value than a *pound* of *lead*.

Wither

Wither having been actively concerned in the
Civil Wars, his character as a Poet, as well as a
Man, is stigmatized in the true spirit of Party
Rage: a stronger testimony cannot be given of
this blindness of Prejudice, than the vile GRUB-
STREET, *Taylor the water poet*, being set in com-
petition to *Wither:* we have now little concern
with *Wither's* personal character, but candour will
hesitate to join in condemnation of the *Man*, when
the *Poet* is so unjustly arraigned; more especially
as He was repeatedly thrown into prison for *His
Satires:* and the last time confined in New-Gate, at
above 70 years of age, for a MS *general Satire,*
seized in his own possession, and construed into a
libel against the House of Commons, without
hearing his defence, but garbling his MS to find
exceptionable parts: *This* and *all* His *other Satires*
were *general:* Thank God the Revolution has
banished from this Country, the oppression of
such Tyranical Power! and it is to be hoped we
shall never be so wanting to ourselves as to bring
it forth again from its lurking Place, by giving
the

the trial, out of our own hands by juries, into those of any Judges whatever: if a Jury gives an *improper verdict* it is confined to the *single case* only, but the determination of Judges, whether in the House of Parliament or on the bench, is made a *precedent* of *Injustice.*

According to *Pope,* there is more offence in *general* than in *personal Satire*

    " The fewer still you name, you wound the more,
    " *Bond* is but one, but *Harpax* is a score."

it is not wonderful that profligate individuals should resent *general satire,* but that there should be such prostitution and perversion of Public Justice, to punish *It* as an offence, is beyond credibility, if the evidence was not uncontrovertible.

General Satires are *Moral Essays,* which come, as Lord Bacon expresses it, home to every Man's heart and bosom; and al.ho' they admit fewer Poetical

B 3   Ideas,

Ideas, than almost any other species of writing, still
Wither has introduced much *Poetical* imagery into
his Satires. They are written in rime, in Heroick
Verse of *ten syllables*; and *Wither's* Verse will *gain*
more by being compared with *Donne*, his immediate
Predecessor, than it will *lose* by a comparison, with
Dryden or *Pope:* altho' *Wither's* JUVENILIA were
published several years before *Dryden* was born.

Pope has said

———— Dryden taught to join,
The varying verse, the full refounding line,
The long majestic march, and energy divine.

but the claim of having *first* deserved this character,
must be granted to *Wither*, altho' it be allowed *He*,
more even than *Dryden*,

———————— " wanted, or forgot,"
What Pope calls
" The last and greatest art, the art to blot."

" *Fair*

" *Fair Virtue*, The *Miſtreſs* of *Philarete*," if not
the *firſt*, appears to be one of *Wither's earlieſt* perfor-
mances. It ſeems to be alluded to in " Abuſes
Stript and Whipt," in the early editions, under
the name of " Aretophil's Complaint;" and in
ſubſequent, under that of "Philarete's Complaint:"
In this Poem of " Fair Virtue," *Wither* has given
a moſt elegant deſcription of Woman, in perſon,
mind, and behaviour.

The Introduction faithfully ſays " Hereby thoſe
" Women, who deſire to be truly beloved, may
" know what makes them ſo to be, and ſeek to
" acquire thoſe accompliſhments of the Mind,
" which may endear them, when the ſweeteſt
" features of a beautiful face ſhall be converted into
" deformity.—Here it ſhall appear, that he who
" was able to conceive the moſt excellent pleaſ-
" ingneſs, which could be apprehended in a
" corporeal Beauty; found it (even when he was
" moſt enamoured with it) far ſhort of that unex-
" preſſible

" preffible fweetnefs, which he difcovered in a
" virtuous and well tempered Difpofition."

There cannot be a properer Introduction to
This Poem in praife of *Female Excellence*, than fome
lines take from it.

Look on *Moon*, on *Stars*, on *Sun*,
All *God's Creatures* over-run;
See, if all of them prefents,
To your mind, fuch fweet contents;
Or, if you, from them can take
Ought that may a Beauty make,
Shall one half fo pleafing prove,
As is *Hers*, whom you do love.
For, indeed, if there had been
Other Mortal Beauties feen,
Objects for the love of man,
Vain was Their Creation then.
Yea, if this could well be granted,
Adam might his *Eve* have wanted.

But a Woman is the Creature,
Whofe proportion with our nature
Beft agrees, and whofe perfections,
Sympathize with our affections:
And not only, find our fenfes
Pleafure in their excellencies;
But our Reafon alfo knows
Sweetnefs in them, that outgoes
Human wit to comprehend ;
Much more, truely, to commend.

The Poem, " *Fair Virtue*," is introduced by a
very tender Addrefs to His Miftrefs, of which the
following are fome of the Stanzas.

Hail, thou faireft of all Creatures,
Upon whom the Sun doth fhine:
Model of all rareft Features,
And Perfections moft divine.
    Thrice all-hail: and bleffed be
    Thofe that love and honour Thee.

This

This, thy *Picture*, therefore shew I
Naked unto every eye,
Yet no fear of *Rival* know I,
Neither touch of *Jealousie*;
    For, the more make love to Thee,
    I the more shall pleafed be.

I, am no *Italian* lover,
That will mewe Thee in a Jayle;
But, thy *Beautie* I difcover,
English-like, without a vail,
    If, Thou mayft be won away;
    Win and wear Thee he that may.

Yet, in this thou mayft believe me;
(So indifferent tho' I feem)
Death with tortures would not grieve me,
More than lofs of thy efteem,
    For, if VIRTUE me forfake;
    All, a fcorn of me will make.

                      Then,

Then, as I on Thee relying
Do no changing feare in Thee:
So, by my defects supplying,
From all changing, keep Thou me.
    That, unmatched we may prove,
    Thou, for *Beautie*; I, for *Love*.

He commences the Poem with a description of
the *Scene*, which is almost the only thing that is
Pastoral * in the whole piece; some Ladies
overhearing him singing, are led by the voice to
the Place of his retirment; He invites them to
an Arbour, where after exchanging Compliments,
They urge him to sing: he at first excuses himself;
but, being further urged, He complies. He then
changes the measure from the *heroick* to the
lyrick.

You,

---

* A dignified Author, who has given *part* of the
Sonnet " *Hence ye Syrens leave me*," COLDLY calls
" The Mistress of Philarete" a *long Pastoral Piece*.

You, that at a blush can tell,
Where the best perfections dwell;
And the substance can conjecture,
By a shadow, or a Picture:
Come, and try, if you by this,
Know my *Mistress*, who she is.

After inviting every thing to hearken, He con‑
cludes his invocation.

Lastly; you that will (I know)
Hear me wh'er you should or no,
You; that seek to turn all flowers,
By your Breath's infectious powers,
Into such rank lothsome weeds
As your dunghill nature breeds.
Let your hearts be chaste, or here,
Come not, till you purge them clear.
Mark; and mark then, what is worst;
For whate'er it seem at first;

If

If you bring a modeft mind,
You fhall nought immodeft find,
But, if any too fevere,
Hap to lend a partial ear;
Or, out of his blindnefs yawn,
Such a word, as *oh prophane!*
Let him know thus much from me,
If here's ought prophane, 'tis He,
Who applies thefe excellencies,
Only to the touch of fenfes;
And, dim-fighted, cannot fee
Where the foul of this, may be.

A number of Sonnets are introduced, too many to be given here, but a few extracts may not be amifs

Sad *Eyes* what do you ail
To be thus ill difpofed?
Why doth your fleeping fail,
Now all mens elfe are clofed?

Was't

Was't I, that ne'er did bow
In any fervile duty;
And will you make me now,
A Slave to Love and Beauty?

    Shall then in earneft truth,
    My careful eyes obferve Her?
    Shall I confume my youth,
    And fhort my time to ferve Her?
Shall I, beyond my ftrength,
Let Paffion's torments prove me,
To hear her fay, at length,
Away, I cannot love Thee?

    Oh, rather let me dye,
    Whilft I thus gentle find her,
    'Twere worfe than death, if I
    Should find fhe proves unkinder.
One frown, (tho' but in jeft)
Or one unkindnefs, fained,
Would rob me of more reft,
Then e'er could be regained.

                    But

But, in her eyes I find
Such figns of Pity moving;
She cannot be unkind;
Nor err, nor faile in loving.
And, on her forehead, this,
Seems written to relieve me;
My heart no joy fhall mifs,
That Love or fhe can give me.

———————

And this fhall be the worft,
Of all that can betide me;
If I, like fome accurft,
Should find my hopes deride me.
My Cares will not be long,
I know which way to mend them;
I'll think, who did the wrong,
Sigh, break my heart, and end them.

Then

Then the Poet proceeds to the defcription of His
Miftrefs's Perfon:

> Firft, that part fhall be difclos'd
> That's of *Elements* compos'd.

> This pure fubftance is the fame,
> Which the Body we do name:
> Were that, of immortal ftuff;
> 'Tis refin'd and pure enough,
> To be call'd a *Soul*; for fure,
> Many *Souls* are not fo pure.

> In the motion of each part,
> *Nature* feems to ftrive with *Art*,
> Which her gefture moft fhall blefs;
> With the gifts of pleafingnefs.

We will not anticipate the *Poet's* perfect defcription
by fcraps. ——but we cannot refift giving fome
part of the following paffionate and beautiful
Sonnet

When

When *Philomela* with her ſtrains,
 The Spring had welcom'd in;
And Flora to beſtrew the Plains,
 With *Daſies* did begin:
My Love and I (on whom ſuſpicious eyes
 Had ſet a thouſand ſpies)
  To cozen Argus ſtrove;
   And ſeen of none
   We got alone,
  Into a ſhady Grove.

On every buſh the *Eglantine*,
 With leaves perfumed, hung,
The Primroſe made the Hedge-Rows fine,
 The Woods, of Muſick rung.
The Earth, the Air, and all things did conſpire
 To raiſe contentment higher.
  That had I come to wooe:
   Nor means of grace,
   Nor time, nor Place;
  Were wanting thereunto.

With

With hand in hand, alone we walkt,
　　And oft each other ey'd:
Of Love, and Paffions paft, we talkt,
　　Which our poor hearts hath tried.
Our Souls infus'd into each others were,
　　And what may be her care,
　　　　Did my more forrow breed;
　　　　　One mind we bore,
　　　　　One Faith we fwore,
　　　　And both in one agreed.

Her dainty palm I gently preft,
　　And with her lips I plaid,
My Cheek upon her panting breaft,
　　And on her neck I laid,
And yet we had no fenfe of wanton luft;
　　Nor did we then miftruft
　　　　The Poifon in the fweet:
　　　　　Our *Bodies* wrought
　　　　　So clofe, we thought,
　　　　Becaufe our *Souls* fhould meet.

　　　　　　　　　　　But,

But, kiffing and embracing, we
 So long together lay;
Her touches all enflamed me,
 And I began to ftray.
My hands prefum'd fo far, they were too bold.
 My Tongue, unwifely, told,
  How much my Heart was chang'd.
  And Virtue quite
  Was put to flight,
  Or for the time eftrang'd.

Oh! what are we if in our ftrength,
 We over-boldly truft?
The ftrongeft Forts, will yield at length:
 And fo our Virtues muft.
In me no force of Reafon had prevail'd;
 If fhe had alfo fail'd,
  But e'er I further ftray'd,
  She fighing kift,
  My naked wrift;
  And thus, in tears, fhe faid.

     Sweet

Sweet Heart, (quoth she) if in thy breast,
 Those Virtues real be,
Which hitherto thou hast profest,
 And I believ'd in Thee:
Thy self, and Me, oh! seek not to abuse ;
 Whilst Thee I thus refuse
  In hotter flames I fric:
   Yet, let us not,
   Our true love spot,
  Oh! rather let me die.

Are we the two, that have so long,
 Each others loves imbrac't ?
And never did Affection wrong,
 Nor think a thought unchast ?
And shall, oh, shall we now, our matchless joy,
 For one poor touch destroy ?
  And all content forego ?
   Oh! no, my Dear,
   Sweet Heart forbear ;
  I will not lose thee so.

For fhould we do a deed fo bafe,
 (As it can never be)
I could no more have feen thy face,
 Nor wouldft thou look on me.
I fhould of all our Paffions grow afham'd,
 And blufh when thou art nam'd,
  Yea, (though thou conftant wert)
  I being nought,
  A jealous thought,
  Wou'd ftill torment my heart.

What goodly thing do we obtain,
 If I confent to Thee?
Rare Joys we lofe, and what we gain,
 But common pleafures be:
Yea, thofe (fome fay) who are to luft inclin'd,
 Drive love out of the mind;
  And fo much reafon mifs:
  'That they admire,
  What kind of fire,
  A chaft affection is.

No vulgar blifs I aimed at,
    When firft I heard thee wooe:
I'll never prize a man for that,
    Which ev'ry Groom can do.
If that be Love; the bafeft men that be,
    Do love as well as we ;
      Who, if we bear us well,
        Do pafs them then,
          As *Angels*, men
      In glory do excell.

Whilft thus fhe fpake, a cruel band
    Of paffions feiz'd my Soul :
And, what one feemed to command,
    Another did controul.
'Twixt *Good* and *Ill*, I did divided lye.
    But as I rais'd mine eye,
      In her me thought I faw
        Thofe Virtues fhine,
        Whofe Rays Divine,
      Firft gave Defire a Law.

                    With

With that, I felt the blush of shame,
   Into my cheek return ;
And *Love*, did with a chaster flame,
   Within my Bosom burn.
My Soul, her light of Reason had renew'd ;
   And by those beams I view'd,
     How slily Lust ensnares,
      And all the fires,
      Of Ill-Desires,
    I quenched with my tears.

Go *wantons* now, and flout at this
   My Coldness, if you list ;
Vain fools, you never knew the bliss,
   That doth in Love consist,
You sigh, and weep, and labour to enjoy,
   A Shade, a Dream, a Toy.
    Poor Folly you pursue ;
      And are unblest,
      Since every beast,
    In Pleasure equals you.

You never took fo rich content,
  In all your wanton play,
As this to me hath pleafure lent,
  That chaft fhe went away.
For as fome fins, which we committed have ;
  Sharp ftings behind them leave,
    Whereby we vexed are :
      So ill fuppreft,
      Begetteth reft,
    And Peace, without compare.

It would make this too long to recite but a
fmall part of the beauties of this delightful Poem :
The following contains fuch an example to the
Fair Sex, it would be unpardonable to pafs it over.

    By herfelf, fhe hath fuch care,
    That her actions decent are ;
    For, were fhe in fecret hid,
    None might fee her what fhe did ;
    She would do, as if, for Spies,
    Every wall were ftuck with eyes.

And

And be chary of her Honour,
'Caufe the heavens do look upon her;
And, oh, what had power to move,
Flames of Luft, or wanton Love,
So far, to difparage us,
If we all were minded thus?
Thefe are Beauties which fhall laft,
When the crimfon blood fhall waft,
And the fhining hair wax grey,
Or with age be worn away,
Thefe yield pleafures, fuch as might
Be remember'd with delight;
When we gafp our lateft breath,
On the loathed bed of death.

———

Tho' difcreetly fpeak fhe can,
She'll be filent, rather than
Talk when others may be heard:
As if fhe did hate, or fear'd,
Their Condition; who will force
All, to wait on their difcourfe.

D   *Reafon*

Reason hath on her beftowed
More of Knowledge, than fhe owed
To that Sex ; and *Grace* with it,
Doth aright her practice fit.
Yet, hath *Fate* fo framed her,
As fhe may at fometime, err :
But, if e'er her judgment ftray,
'Tis that other women may,
Thofe much pleafing Beauties fee,
Which in yielding Natures be.

————

Should you hear her, once, contend
In difcourfing, to defend
(As fhe can) a doubtful Caufe :
She fuch ftrong pofitions draws
From known Truths, and doth apply,
Reafons with fuch Majeftie :
As if *She*, did undertake,
From fome *Oracle* to fpeak.
And you could not think, what might
Breed more love, or more delight.

Yet,

Yet, if you fhould mark again,
Her difcreet behaviour, when
She finds reafon to repent
Some wrong-pleaded *Argument.*
She fo temper'ately lets all
Her mis-held opinions fall;
And, can with fo much mildnefs bow;
As 'twill more enamour you,
Than Her Knowledge, For, there are
Pleafing fweets without compare
In fuch yieldings; which do prove,
Wit, Humility, and *Love.*

Thefe Sentiments every woman fhould bear in
Her Heart as the Jews did their Phylactarys on
their Foreheads.

Rofes and ¡Lillies are the common ingredients
without which no Poet can paint his Miftrefs;
before we leave this Poem it may be fatisfactory
to fee how *they* are applied.

" On

" On the either fide of this, *
Love's moft lovely profpect is.
Thofe Her fmiling Che ks, whofe colour
Comprehends true *Beauty* fuller,
Than the curiouft mixtures can,
That are made by art of Man.
It is Beauty's *garden-plot,*
Where, as in a *True love knot,*
So, the fnowy Lilly grows,
Mix.d with the Crimfon Rofe,
That as Friends they joined be:
Yet, they feem to difagree,
Whether of the two fhall reign;
And the Lillies oft obtain
Greater fway, unlefs a blufh
Help the Rofes at a pufh.

At the end of This Poem is a " Mifcellany of
Epigrams, Sonnets, &c." As a Specimen of our

---

* Her Nofe.

Author's

Author's manner of treating common ideas, the following may be taken.

"A Sonnet upon a stolen Kifs."

Now gentle Sleep, hath clofed up thofe eyes,
Which waking, kept my boldeft thoughts in awe;
And free accefs, unto that fweet lip, lies,
From whence I long the rofie breath to draw.
Methinks no wrong it were, if I fhould fteal
From thofe two melting Rubies, one poor kifs;
None fees the theft, that would the thief reveal,
Nor rob I her of ought, which fhe can mifs:
Nay, fhould I twenty kiffes take away,
There would be little fign I had done fo;
Why then fhould I this robbery delay?
Oh! fhe may wake, and therewith angry grow.
　　Well, if fhe do, I'll back reftore that one,
　　And twenty hundred thoufand more for loan,

This collection concludes with an elegaic Epiftle of Farewel from an empaffioned Friend to

a married

a married Lady whom He leaves that they might·
·ever be enfnared by their mutual ·tendernefs to·
any improper· behaviour.

Swift Time, that will, by no entreaty, ftay,
Is now gone by, and fummons me away.
And what my grief denies my tongue to do,
My true affection drives my pen unto.
Dear Heart, that day, and that fad hour, is come
In which, thy Face I muft be banifh'd from:
And go to live, where (peradventure) we
Hereafter muft, for aye, divided be.

————

Thofe Parents, that difcreet in loving be,
When on their new-born child a wen they fee,
Which may, (perchance) in aftertime difgrace
The fweet proportion of a lovely face:
(Altho' it wound their fouls to hear the moan,
And fee the tortures of their *pretty-one*)
To weep a little rather are content
Whilft he endures the Surgeon's Inftrument;

Then

Than fuffer that foul blemifh there, to fpread,
Until his face be quite disfigured.
So, we, betwixt whofe fouls thefe is begot,
That fweet babe, Friendfhip, muft beware, no fpot
Through our indulgent indifcretion grow,
That may the beauty of our love o'erthrow :
Let's rather bear a little difcontent,
And learn of Reafon, thofe things to prevent,
Which mar affection. That our Friendfhip may
Waxe firmer, and more love'ly ev'ry day.

———————

Then let us pleafed part ; and tho' the dearnefs
Of our affection, covets both a nearnefs
In *mind* and *body*, let us unwillingly
Beget a virtue of Neceffity.
And fince we muft compelled be to live,
By time and place divided ; let us ftrive
In the defpight of Time and Diftance, fo
That love of Virtue may more perfect grow :
And that this feperation we lament,
May make our meeting fuller of content.

Yea,

Yea, whereas carnal Love, is ever colder,
As Youth decays, and as the flesh grows older;
And, when the body is dissolved, must
Be buried with oblivion in the dust.
We, then shall dearer grow, and this our Love,
Which now imperfect is, shall perfect prove:
For, there's no mortal power can rob true friends,
Of *that* which noblest amity attends,
Nor any seperation that is able,
To make the virtuous Lovers miserable.
Since, when disasters threaten most dejection,
Their Goodness maketh strongest their affection,
And, that which works in others loves denial;
In them, more noble makes it, by the tryal.

'Tis true, that when we part, we know not whether
Those bodies shall, for ever, meet together,
As you have said; yet, wherefore should we grieve,
Since, we a better meeting do believe?
If we did also know, that when we die,
This Love should perish everlastingly,

And

And that we muft, as brutifh creatures do,
Lofe with our bodies, all our dearnefs too,
Our feparation, then, a forrow were,
Which mortal hearts had never power to bear:
But, feeing in the Soul, our Love is plac'd ;
And (feeing) Souls of Death fhall never taft ;
No Death can end our Love. Nay when we die,
Our Souls (that now in chains and fetters lye)
Shall meet more freely, to partake that joy,
Compar'd to which, our Friendfhip's but a toy

Mean while, we, that (together living) may
Through human weakneffes be led aftray:
(And unawares, make that affection foul,
Which Virtue, yet keeps blamclefs in the Soul)
By abfence fhall preferved be, as clean,
As to be kept (in our beft thoughts) we mean,
And, in our pray'ers for each other, fhall
Give, and receive more kindueffes, than all
The world can yield us. And when other men,
Whofe Love is carnal, are tormented when

Death

Death calls them hence, becauſe they robbed be
Of all their hope (for evermore) to ſee
The object of their Love: we ſhall avoid
That bitter anguiſh wherewith they are cloy'd
And, whenſo'er it happens, thou, or I,
Shall feel the time approaching us to die;
It ſhall not grieve us at our lateſt breath,
To mind each other on the bed of death:
Nor will death fear us, cauſe we ſhall perceive
That thoſe contentments, which we had not leave
To take now we are living, ſhall be gain'd
When our unpriſon'd Souls ſhall be unchain'd,
Nay rather wiſh to die, we might poſſeſs
The ſweet fruition of that happineſs,
Which we ſhall then receive, in the perfection
Of Him, that is the fulneſs of Affection.

————

Mean while, you ſtill are dear; yea, live or die,
My Soul ſhall love you everlaſtingly.
And how ſo'er, there ſeem ſuch cauſe of ſorrow;
Yet, thoſe that part, and think to meet to-morrow,
Death

Death may divide to-night; and, as before,
Their Fear was lefs, their Grief will be the more,
Since therefore, whether far I live, or nigh,
There is in meeting an incertainty :
Let us, for that which fureft is, provide :
Part like thofe Friends, whom nothing can divide;
And, fince we Lovers firft became, that we,
Might to our power, each others comfort be ;
Let's not the fweetnefs of our love deftroy ;
But, turn thofe weepings into tears of Joy:
On which condition, I do give thee, *this* ;
To be both *mine*, and *Sorrow's* parting-kifs.

It is not propofed to cite the *Poems* in the *Order*
they ftand in the *Juvenilia* ; but to keep his Satyres apart.

The next in date then, to " *Fair Virtue*, The Miftrefs
" of Philarete," will be " Prince Henry's Obfequies."
This is fo different from the common ftile of Court
Funeral Elegies that it would be unpardonable to
confign

confign it to that oblivion which fuch pieces ge-
nerally deferve. We fhall however only give the
32 Elegy; tho' we cannot omit referring particularly to the addrefs to the Queen, in Elegy 6; and
to the 36 Elegy, expreffing his own feelings, and
the Character of Prince Henry.

For underftanding the following, it is neceffary
to mention, that Prince Henry's body embalmed
was carried in Funeral Proceffion.

Elegy 32.

Then, as he paft along you might efpy
How the griev'd Vulgar that fhed many a tear,
Caft after, an unwilling parting eye,
As loth to lofe the fight they held fo dear;
When they had loft the figure of his face,
Then they beheld his robes; his chariot then,
Which being hid, their look aim'd at the Place,
Still longing to behold him once again :

But

. But when he was quite paſt, and they could find,
No object to employ their ſight upon,
Sorrow became more buſy with the mind,
And drew an army of ſad paſſions on ;
   Which made them ſo particularly moan,
   Each amongſt thouſands ſeem'd as if alone.

Altho' there is no Edition mentioned of the
Epithalamia of an earlier date than 1622, yet as
the *Princeſs Elizabeth's* Marriage, which is the ſub-
ject of them, happened in 1612, it is probable
they were printed before 1622.　In the concluding
part, are ſome *Epigrams concerning Marriage*, of
which the following is the 3ᵈ.

Soldier ; of thee I aſk, for thou canſt beſt,
Having known *Sorrow*, judge of *Joy* and *Reſt* :
What greater bliſs, than after all thy harms,
To have a Wife that's fair, and lawful thine ;
And lying priſon'd 'twixt her ivory arms,
There tell what Thou has 'ſcapt by Powers divine ?

How many, round thee, thou haſt murther'd ſeen;
How oft thy ſoul hath been near hand expiring,
How many times thy fleſh hath wounded been:
Whilſt ſhe thy fortune and thy worth admiring,
With joy of health, and pity of thy pain;
Doth weep and kiſs, and kiſs and weep again.

Epigram 6.

Long did I wonder, and I wonder much,
Rome's Church ſhould from her Clergy take that due;
Thought I, why ſhould ſhe that contentment grutch?
What, doth ſhe all with continence indue?
No: But why then are they debar'd that State?
Is ſhe become a Foe unto her own?
Doth ſhe the members of her body hate?
Or is it for ſome other cauſe unſhown?
Oh yes: *they find a woman's lips ſo dainty;*
They tye themſelves from one, 'cauſe they'll have twenty.

The next piece is " The Shepherd's Hunting"
written in the *Marſhalſea* whilſt he was confined
there

there for His *former* Book " Abufes ftript and " whipt." It is in dialogues between him and fome of his Friends who vifit him: It is pleafing to fee with what fortitude he bears his fate.

A. Are Prifons then grown Places of Delight?
P. T'is as the *confcience* of the *Prifoner* is,
    The very *grates* are able to affright
    The guilty man, that knows his deeds amifs.

———

All outward *Pleafures* are exiled quite,
  And it is nothing (of itfelf) but This :
Abhorred lonenefs, darknefs, fadnefs, pains,
Num'n-cold,fharp-hunger,fcorching thirft &chains.

Some Sonnets are introduced, in one of them he moft pathetically defcribes his fituation.

I that ere'ft-while the Worlds fweet Air did draw
(Grac'd by the Faireft ever Mortal faw)
Now clofely pent, with walls of ruth-lefs ftone ;
Confume my days, and nights, and all alone.

When

When I was wont to fing of Shepherd's Loves,
My walks were fields, and downs, and hills and groves;
But now (alas) fo ftrict is my hard doom,
Fields, downs, hills, groves and all's but one poor room.

Each morn as foon as day-light did appear,
With Nature's mufick, Birds would charm mine ear;
Which now, inftead of their melodious ftrains
Hear ratling fhackles, gyves, and bolts, and chains.

But, tho' that all the worlds delight forfake me,
I have a *Mufe* and fhe fhall mufick make me:
Whofe airy Note, in fpight of clofeft cages,
Shall give content to me and after ages.

Nor do I pafs for all this outward ill,
My heart's the fame and undejected ftill;
And, which is more than fome in freedom win,
I have true reft, and peace, and joy within.

And then my mind, that fpight of prifon's free,
When e'er fhe pleafes, any where can be;

She's

She's in an hour, in France, Rome, Turky, Spain,
In Earth, in Hell, in Heaven and here again,

Yet there's another comfort in my woe,
My caufe is fpread, and all the world may know,
My faults no more but fpeaking truth and reafon ;
No debt, nor theft, nor murther, rape nor treafon.

Nor fhall my foes with all their might and power,
Wipe out their fhame, nor yet this fame of our ;
Which when they find, they fhall my fate envie,
Till they grow lean, and mad, and fick and die,

Then tho' my body here in prifon rot,
And my wrong'd *Satyres* feem a-while forgot :
Yet when both Fame, and life hath left thefe men,
My verfe, and I'll revive, and live again.

So then enclos'd, I bear afflictions load,
But with more true content than fome abroad ;
For whilft their thoughts, do feel my *Scourge's* fting,
In bonds I'll leap, and dance, and laugh and fing.

E 3   A. Why

A. Why now I fee thou droops't not with thy care,

———————

All that did truely know thee, did conceive,
Thy actions with thy fpirit ftill agreed ;
Their good conceit thou doft no whit bereave,
But fheweft that thou art ftill thyfelf indeed,
If that thy Mind to *bafenefs* now defcends,
Thoul't injure *Virtue*, and deceive thy Friends,

W. Alexis, he will injure VIRTUE much,
But more his *Friends*, and moft of all *himfelf*,
If on that common *bar* his mind but touch,
It wrecks his *Fame* upon *Difgrace's fhelf.*
Whereas if Thou fteer on that happy courfe,
Which in thy juft adventure is begun ;
No *thwarting Tide*, nor *adverfe Blaft* fhall force
Thy *Bark* without The CHANNELS bounds to run.

Perhaps there never was a more perfect Metaphor; but a Man muft be a Seaman to feel the full force of it.

In another *Sonnet* in this Piece he has made a moft happy and poetical allufion to the *day of*
Judgement :

Judgement: it is an addrefs to his own Soul, and begins

Now that my body, dead-alive,
Bereav'd of comfort, lyes in thrall,
Do Thou, my Soul, begin to thrive,
And unto Honey, turn this Gall:
   So fhall we both through outward woe,
   The way to inward comfort know.

As, to the Flefh we food do give;
To keep in us this Mortal breath:
So, Souls on Meditation live,
And fhun thereby immortal death:
   Nor art thou ever nearer reft,
   Than when thou finds't me moft oppreft,

Firft think, my Soul; if I have foes
That take a pleafure in my care,
And to procure thofe outward woes,
Have thus entrapt me unaware:

Thou

Thou fhould'ft by much more careful be,
Since greater Foes lye wait for thee.

Or, when through me, thou fee'ft a Man
Condemn'd unto a mortal death,
How fad he looks, how pale, how wan,
Drawing with fear his panting breath :
 Think, if in that, fuch grief you fee,
 How, fad will, Go ye cursed ! be.

Again, when he that fear'd to die,
(*Paſt hope*) doth fee his *pardon* brought,
Read but the *joy* that's in his *eye*,
And then convey it to thy thought :
 There think, betwixt thy heart and thee,
 How fweet will, Come ye blessed ! be,

The other *Sonnet* in this piece is a dialogue with
two Friends who come to confole him.

W.

W. Shepherd, would thefe gates were ope,
 Thou migh'ft take with us thy Fortune.

P. No, I'll make this narrow fcope,
 (Since my Fate doth fo importune)
  Means unto a wider hope.

C. Would thy Shepherdefs were here,
 Who beloved, loves fo dearly ?

P. Not for both your Flocks I fwear,
 And the gain they yield you yearly,
  Would I fo much wrong my Dear.

Yet, to me, nor to this Place,
Would fhe now be long a Stranger:
She would hold it no difgrace,
(If fhe fear'd not more my danger)
 Where I am, to fhew her Face.

W. Shepherd, we would wifh no harms,
 But fomething that might content thee.

P, Wifh me then within her arms;
 And that wifh will ne'er repent me,
  If your wifhes might prove charms.

         W.

W. Be thy Prifon,—Her Embrace,

    Be thy Air—Her fweeteft breathing.

C. Be thy Profpect—Her fweet Face,

    For each look, a Kifs bequeathing,

        And appoint thyfelf the Place.

We fhall conclude this Poem with his exclamation in favour of Poetry.

But (alas) my Mufe is flow,

For thy place fhe flags too low :

Yea, the more's her haplefs fate,

Her fhort wings were clipt of late,

And, poor I, her fortune ruing,

Am myfelf put up a muing.

And tho', for her fake, I'm croft,

Tho' my beft hopes I have loft,

And knew fhe would make my trouble,

Ten times more than ten times double ;

I fhould love, and keep her too,

Spight of all the World could do.

                      For

For tho' banifh'd from my flocks,
And confin'd within thefe Rocks;
Here I wafte away the light,
And confume the fullen night,
She doth for my comfort ftay,
And keeps many cares away.
Tho' I mifs the flowr'y Fields
With thofe fweets the Spring-tide yields;

Tho' of all thofe pleafures paft,
Nothing now remains at laft,
But Remembrance (poor relief)
That more makes, than mends my grief
She's my mind's companion ftill,
Maugre Envy's evil will.
She doth tell me where to borrow
Comfort in the midft of forrow,
Makes the defolateft place
To her prefence be a grace ;
And the blackeft difcontents
To be pleafing ornaments,

In

In my former days of blifs,
Her divine fkill taught me this,
That from every thing I faw,
I could fome invention draw:
And raife Pleafure to her height,
Thro' the meaneft object's fight,
By the murmur of a fpring,
Or the leaft bough's rufteling:
By a daifie whofe leaves, fpread,
Shut when *Titan* goes to bed;
Or a fhady bufh or tree,
She would more infufe in me,
Than all nature's beauties can,
In fome other wifer man.
By her help I alfo now,
Make this churlifh place, allow
Some things that may fweeten gladnefs,
In the very gall of fadnefs.
The dull lonenefs, the black fhade,
That thefe hanging vaults have made,
The ftrange Mufick of the waves,
Beating on thefe hollow caves,

This

This black Den which Rocks embosse
Over grown with eldest Mofs.
The rude *Portals* that give light,
More to *Terror* than *Delight*.
This my Chamber of *Neglect*,
Wall'd about with *Difrefpect*,
From all thefe and this dull air,
A fit object for Defpair,
She hath taught me, by her might,
To draw comfort and delight.
Therefore *thou beft earthly blifs*,
I will cherifh thee for this.
Poefy ; thou fweetest content
That e'er Heav'n to Mortals lent ;
Tho' they, as a trifle leave thee,
Whofe dull thought cannot conceive thee,
Tho' thou be to them a fcorn,
That to nought but Earth are born :
Let my Life no longer be
Than I am, in love with Thee

F   " The

" The Shepherd's Hunting" is followed by
" *Fidelia*" a moſt paſſionate and elegant Elegaick
Poem ſaid to be a Fragment ; It is an Epiſtle from
a modeſt woman to her *ſuppoſed* inconſtant Lover,
in which are expreſſed (as the Introduction ſays)
" the height of Female Paſſions, ſo far as they ſeem
" to agree with reaſon, and keep within ſuch de-
" cent bounds as becometh their ſex."

But, ſith thy *Love* grows cold, and thou unkind,
Be not diſpleas'd I ſomewhat breathe my mind ;
I am in hope, my words may prove a mirrour,
Whereon thou looking, mayſt behold thine error.
And yet, the Heaven, and my ſad heart, doth know
How griev'd I am, and with what feeling woe
My Mind is tortured, to think that I
Should be the brand of thy diſloyalty :
Or, live to be the Author of a line
That ſhall be printed with a fault of Thine ;

———————

Oh that *Love's* Patron, or ſome ſacred *Muſe*,
Amongſt my *paſſions*, would ſuch art infuſe,

My

My well-fram'd words, and airy fighs might prove
The happy blafts to re-inflame thy love.
Or, at leaft, touch thee with thy fault fo near,
That thou might'ft fee thou wrong'ft who held thee dear:
Seeing, confefs the fame, and fo abhor it,
Abhorring, pity, and repent thee for it.

But, who can fay, what we fhall live to do ?
I have believed, and let in, liking too;
And that fo far, I cannot yet fee how
I may fo much as hope, to help it now ;
Which makes me think, whate'er we *women* fay,
Another mind will come another day.
And that men may, to things unhop'd for climb,
Who watch for *Opportunity* and *Time*.
For 'tis well known, we were not made of clay,
Of fuch coarfe, and ill-temper'd ftuff as they.
For he that fram'd us of their flefh, did deign
When 'twas at beft, to new-refin't again.
Which makes us ever fince the kinder *Creatures*,
Of far more flexible and yielding *Natures*,

F 2 And

And as we oft excell in outward parts,
So we have nobler and more gentle Hearts.

———— —

Fool that I am, I fear my guerdon's juſt,
In that I knew this, and preſum'd to truſt,
And yet (alas) for ought that I could tell,
One ſpark of goodneſs in the world might dwell :
And then, I thought, if ſuch a thing might be,
Why might not that one ſpark remain in Thee ?

————

But now I've try'd, my bought experience knows,
They oft are worſt, that make the faireſt ſhows.
And howſoe'er men fain an outward grieving,
'Tis neither worth reſpecting, nor believing :
For, ſhe that doth one to her mercy take,
Warms in her boſom but a frozen ſnake :
Which heated with her favours, gathers ſenſe,
And ſtings her to the heart in recompence.

————

Where's ſhe did more delight in ſprings and rills ?
Where's ſhe that walk'd more, Groves, or Downs or Hills?

Or

Or could, by such fair artless prospect, more
Add by conceit, to her Contentment's store
Than I; whilst Thou wer't true, and with thy Graces
Didst give a pleasing presence to those Places?
But now *what is!* *what was* hath overthrown,
My Rose-deckt allies now with rue are strewn;
And from those flowers that honey'd use to be,
I suck nought now but Juice to poison me.

———— —

How fair (think I) would this sweet place appear,
If he I love, were present with me here.
Nay, every several object that I see,
Doth severally (methinke) remember Thee.
But the delight I us'd from thence to gather,
I now exchange for cares, and seek them rather.

———— —

There I beheld, what on a thin rin'd tree,
Thou hadst engraven for the love of me;
When we two, all one, in heat of day,
With chast embraces drove swift hours away.
Then I remember too (unto my smart)
How loath we were, when time compell'd to part;

How

How cunningly thy *Paſſions* thou couldſt fain,
In taking leave, and coming back again :
So oft, until (as ſeeming to forget
We were departing) down again we ſet ?
And freſhly in that ſweet diſcourſe went on,
Which now, I almoſt faint to think upon.

— ———

Well Love (ſaidſt thou) ſince neither ſigh nor vow,
Nor any ſervice may avail me now :
Since neither the recital of my ſmart,
Nor thoſe ſtrong *paſſions* that aſſail my heart;
Nor any thing may move thee to belief
Of theſe my ſufferings, or to grant relief :
Since there's no comfort, nor deſert, that may
Get me ſo much as *Hope* of what I pray ;
Sweet Love farewell; farewell fair beauty's light,
And every pleaſing object of the ſight :
My poor deſpairing Heart here biddeth you,
And all content, for evermore, adieu.

Then, ev'n as thou ſeem'ſt ready to depart ;
Reaching that hand, which after gave my Heart,

(And

(And thinking this sad *farewell* did proceed
From a *sound* Breaſt, but truely mov'd indeed)
I ſtayed thy departing from me ſo,
Whilſt I ſtood mu'e with *ſorrow*, thou for *ſhew*.
And the mean while as I beheld thy look,
My Eye th' impreſſion of ſuch *Pity* took,
That, with the ſtrength of *Paſſion* overcome,
A deep-fetcht ſigh my heart came breathing from.
Whereat thou (ever wiſely uſing this
To take advantage when it offered is)
Renewds't thy ſuit to me, who did afford
Conſent, in ſilence firſt, and then in word.

The Dyal-needle, tho' it ſenſe doth want,
Still bends to the beloved *Adamant* ;
Lift the one up, the other upward tends ;
If this fall down, that preſently deſcends :
Turn but about the ſtone, the ſteel turns too,
Then ſtraight returns, if ſo the other do ;
And, if it ſtay, with trembling keeps one place,
As if it (panting) long'd for an embrace.
So was't with me : for, if thou merry wert,
That mirth of thine mov'd joy within my heart :

I ſigh'd

I figh'd too, when thou didſt figh or frown:
When thou wert ſick, thou haſt perceiv'd me ſwoon;
And being ſad, have oft with forc'd delight,
Striv'd to give *thee* content beyond my might.
When thou wouldſt talk, then have I talk'd with thee,
And ſilent been, when thou wouldſt ſilent be.
If thou abroad didſt go, with joy I went;
If home thou lov'dſt, at home was my content.
Yea, what did to my *Nature* diſagree,
I could make pleaſing, 'cauſe it pleaſed Thee.

There ſome peculiar thing innated is
That bears an uncontrouled ſway in this;
And nothing but itſelf, knows how to fit
The mind, with that which beſt ſhall ſuit with it;
Then why ſhould *Parents* thruſt themſelves into
What they want warrant for, and power to do?
How is it they are ſo foregetful grown,
Of thoſe conditions, that were once their own?
Do they ſo doat amidſt their wits perfection,
To think that age and youth hath like affection?

(When

(When they do fee 'mong thofe of equal years,
One hateth what another moft endears,)
Or do they think their wifdoms can invent
A thing to give, that's greater than Content?
No, neither fhall they wrap us in fuch blindnefs,
To make us think the fpight they do, is kindnefs,
For as I would advife no Child to ftray
From the leaft duty that he ought to pay:
So would I alfo have him wifely know,
How much that duty is, which he doth owe;
That knowing what doth unto both belong,
He may do them their right, himfelf no wrong.

————————

Children owe much, I muft confefs 'tis true,
And a great debt is to the *Parents* due;
Yet if they have not fo much power to crave,
But in their own defence, the lives they gave,
How much *lefs* then fhould they become fo cruel
As to take from them the high priz'd Jewell
Of Liberty in choice, whereon depends
The main Contentment that Heaven here lends?

. Worth

Worth Life or Wealth, nay far more worth than either
Or twenty thousand lives put all together.

Then hasten *Dear*, if to my end it be,
It shall be welcome, 'cause it comes from Thee.
If to renew my comfort ought be sent,
Let me not lose a minute of *Content*,
The precious *Time* is short and will away,
Let us enjoy each other while we may.
Cares thrive, *Age* creepeth on, *Men* are but shades,
Joys lessen, *Youth* decays, and *Beauty* fades;
New turns come on, the old returneth never,
If we let our go past, 'tis past for ever.

" *Wither's Motto*" *nec habeo, nec careo, nec curo.*
" Nor *have* I, nor *want* I, nor *care* I," is a spirited
Poem which shews great independance of mird;
and has many *Poetical Beauties* in *it*; but we shall
not give any quotations: Nor of *His Satyres* which
are " *Abufes ftript and whipt*" in 2 *Books*;
Book 1 contains " The Occasion," " The In-
" troduction" "Of Man" Satyre 1. Of fond Love
2. Luft,

2. Luft, 3. Hate, 4. Envy, 5. Revenge, 6. Choler,
7. Jealoufy, 8. Covetoufnefs, 9. Ambition, 10. Fear,
11. Defpair, 12. Hope, 13. Compaffion, 14. Cruelty,
15. Joy, 16. Sorrow "The Conclufion." *Book* 2
Sat. 1. Vanity, 2. Inconftancy, 3. Weaknefs,
4. Prefumption " *The Scourge. Epigrams* to
Perfons to whom the Author gave his Books.

" *Satyre to the King*" whilft in prifon, being a
fpirited defence of Himfelf, which had fo good ef-
fect as to get his releafe.

Having now given a fummary Account of the
Contents of *Wither's Juvenilia*, we fhall conclude
with a lift of fuch other of *his Works*, as are known
to the Editor to exift at prefent: expreffing where
fuch may be found, as are not in his own poffeffion.
B. M denoting The *Britifh Mufeum*, B. The
Bodleian Library, and H. The Collection of Mr.
William Herbert, the indefatigable Editor of the
New Edition of *Ames's Typography*.

1614 Eclcgues

1614 Eclogues by Mr. Brook, Mr. Wither, and
    Mr. Davis - - 8? - B
    N. B. Wood says " at the End of *Brown's
Shepherd's Pipe.*" there is however only one commendatory Poem by *Wither*, and another is prefixed to *Brown's Britannia's Pastoral*.
1619 Preparation for the Psalter - f? - B
1620 Exercises on the 1st Psalm   8? - D
1628 Britain's Remembrancer - 12?
1634 Poem on Usury, in Blaxton's English Usurer.
1635 Wither's Emblems - - f?
1641 Haleluiah - - 12? - H
1643 Campo Musæ - - 8?
1643 Wither's Remembrancer (*Quere* if this is not
    by his Antagonists) - - B. M
1645 Vox Pacifica - - - - H
1645 The Great Assises holden in Parnassus - B
1652 The Dark Lanthorn - - - H
1653 Ditto, and Perpetual Parliament 12?
1653 Westrow Reviv'd, a Funeral Poem 8? B. M
1659 Salt upon Salt - - 8? - H
1660 Fides Anglicana - - 9? - H
1660 Furor Poeticus - - - H
1660 Speculum Speculativum, or Considering } 8?
    Glass; and Shepherd of Bledonham }
1661 Joco-serio - - - - H
1661 A Triple Paradox - - - H
    Lottery - - - f? - H
1661 The Prisoner's Plea, *prose* 8?
1664 Tuba Pacifica - - 8?
1666 Sighs for the Pitchers - 8?
1668 Nil Ultra
1669 Fragmenta Prophetica, same as above with new Title
1688 Divine Poems by way of Paraphrase on the Ten
    Commandments - - 8?
no year. The Scholar's Purgatory, *prose* 8? B. M
Ditto Apologetical Remonstrance against Richard
    Onslow - - - 4? B. M

www.ingramcontent.com/pod-product-compliance
Lightning Source LLC
Chambersburg PA
CBHW022015050726
47499CB00007BA/2653